WHAT SAY INDIA

NARESH

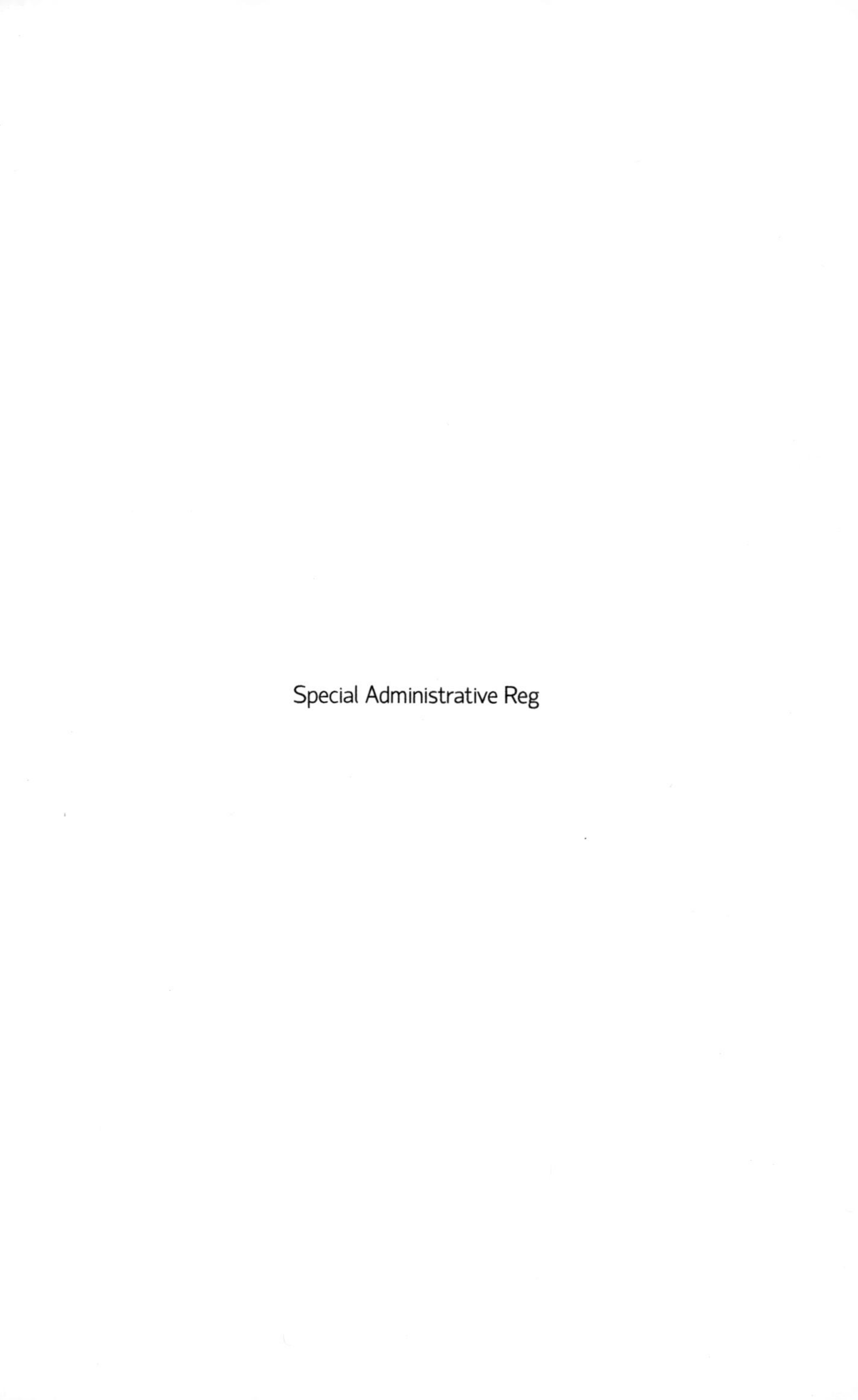
Special Administrative Reg

Contents

Foreword

The government cons

Preface

nment, respond to stimuli, reproduce and evolve. Other definitions sometimes include non-cellular life forms such as viruses and viro

Acknowledgements

between 1958 and 1961, mostly from starvation.[113][114] In 1966, Mao and his allies launched the Cultural Revolution, sparking

CHAPTER ONE

Life

Life

Life is a characteristic that distinguishes physical entities that have biological processes, such as signaling and self-sustaining processes, from those that do not, either because such functions have ceased (they have died) or because they never had such functions and are classified as inanimate. Various forms of life exist, such as plants, animals, fungi, protists, archaea, and bacteria. Biology is the science that studies life.

There is currently no consensus regarding the definition of life. One popular definition is that organisms are open systems that maintain homeostasis, are composed of cells, have a life cycle, undergo metabolism, can grow, adapt to their environment, respond to stimuli, reproduce and evolve. Other definitions sometimes include non-cellular life forms such as viruses and viroids.

Abiogenesis is the natural process of life arising from non-living matter, such as simple organic compounds. The prevailing scientific hypothesis is that the transition from non-living to living entities was not a single event, but a gradual process of increasing complexity. Life on Earth first appeared as early as 4.28 billion years ago, soon after ocean formation 4.41 billion years ago, and not long after the formation of Earth 4.54 billion years ago.[1][2][3][4] The earliest known life forms are bacteria.[5][6] Life on Earth is probably descended from an RNA world,[7] although RNA-based life may not have been the first life to have existed.[8][9] Metal-Binding Proteins that allowed biological electron transfer may have evolved from minerals.[10] The classic 1952 Miller–Urey experiment and similar research demonstrated that most amino acids, the chemical constituents of the proteins used in all living organisms, can be synthesized from inorganic compounds under conditions intended to replicate those of the early Earth. Complex organic molecules occur in the Solar System and in interstellar space, and these molecules may have provided starting material for the development of life on Earth.[11][12][13][14]

Since its primordial beginnings, life on Earth has changed its environment on a geologic time scale, but it has also adapted to survive in most ecosystems and conditions. Some microorganisms, called extremophiles, thrive in physically or geochemically extreme environments that are detrimental to most other life on Earth. The cell is considered the structural and functional unit of life.[15][16] There are two kinds of cells, prokaryotic and eukaryotic, both of which consist of cytoplasm enclosed within a membrane and contain many biomolecules such as proteins and nucleic acids. Cells reproduce through a process of cell division, in which the parent cell divides into two or more daughter cells.

In the past, there have been many attempts to define what is meant by "life" through obsolete concepts such as Odic force, hylomorphism, spontaneous generation and vitalism, that have now been disproved by biological discoveries. Aristotle is considered to be the first person to classify organisms. Later, Carl Linnaeus introduced his system of binomial nomenclature for the classification of species. Eventually new groups and categories of life were discovered, such as cells and microorganisms, forcing significant revisions of the structure of relationships between living organisms. Though currently only known on Earth, life need not be restricted to it, and many scientists speculate in the existence of extraterrestrial life. Artificial life is a computer simulation or human-made reconstruction of any aspect of life, which is often used to examine systems related to natural life.

Death is the permanent termination of all biological processes which sustain an organism, and as such, is the end of its life. Extinction is the term describing the dying-out of a group or taxon, usually a species. Fossils are the preserved remains or traces of organisms.

Contents

1 Definitions1.1 Biology

The definition of life has long been a challenge for scientists and philosophers.[17][18][19] This is partially because life is a process, not a substance.[20][21][22] This is complicated by a lack of knowledge of the characteristics of living entities, if any, that may have developed outside of Earth.[23][24] Philosophical definitions of life have also been put forward, with similar difficulties on how to distinguish living things from the non-living.[25] Legal definitions of life have also been described and debated, though these generally focus on the decision to declare a human dead, and the legal ramifications of this decision.[26] As many as 123 definitions of life have been compiled.[27] One definition seems to be favored by NASA: "a self-sustaining chemical system capable of Darwinian evolution".[28][29][30][31] More simply, life is, "matter that can reproduce itself and evolve as survival dictates".[32][33][34]

Biology

See also: Organism

The characteristics of life

Since there is no unequivocal definition of life, most current definitions in biology are descriptive. Life is considered a characteristic of something that preserves, furthers or reinforces its existence in the given environment. This characteristic exhibits all or most of the following traits:[19][35][36][37][38][39][40]

Homeostasis: regulation of the internal environment to maintain a constant state; for example, sweating to reduce temperature

Organization: being structurally composed of one or more cells – the basic units of life

Metabolism: transformation of energy by converting chemicals and energy into cellular components (anabolism) and decomposing organic matter (catabolism). Living things require energy to maintain internal organization (homeostasis) and to produce the other phenomena associated with life.

Growth: maintenance of a higher rate of anabolism than catabolism. A growing organism increases in size in all of its parts, rather than simply accumulating matter.

Adaptation: the ability to change over time in response to the environment. This ability is fundamental to the process of evolution and is determined by the organism's heredity, diet, and external factors.

Response to stimuli: a response can take many forms, from the contraction of a unicellular organism to external chemicals, to complex reactions involving all the senses of multicellular organisms. A response is often expressed by motion; for example, the leaves of a plant turning toward the sun (phototropism), and chemotaxis.

Reproduction: the ability to produce new individual organisms, either asexually from a single parent organism or sexually from two parent organisms.

These complex processes, called physiological functions, have underlying physical and chemical bases, as well as signaling and control mechanisms that are essential to maintaining life.

Alternative definitions

See also: Entropy and life

From a physics perspective, living beings are thermodynamic systems with an organized molecular structure that can reproduce itself and evolve as survival dictates.[41][42] Thermodynamically, life has been described as an open system which makes use of gradients in its surroundings to create imperfect copies of itself.[43] Another way of putting this is to define life as "a self-sustained chemical system capable of undergoing Darwinian evolution", a definition adopted by a NASA committee attempting to define life for the purposes of exobiology, based on a suggestion by Carl Sagan.[44][45][46] A major strength of this definition is that it distinguishes life by the evolutionary process rather than its chemical composition.[47]

Others take a systemic viewpoint that does not necessarily depend on molecular chemistry. One systemic definition of life is that living things are self-organizing and autopoietic (self-producing). Variations of this definition include Stuart Kauffman's definition as an autonomous agent or a multi-agent system capable of reproducing itself or themselves, and of completing at least one thermodynamic work cycle.[48] This definition is extended by the apparition of novel functions over time.[49]

Viruses

Main articles: Virus and Virus classification

Adenovirus as seen under an electron microscope

Whether or not viruses should be considered as alive is controversial. They are most often considered as just gene coding replicators rather than forms of life.[50] They have been described as "organisms at the edge of life"[51] because they possess genes, evolve by natural selection,[52][53] and replicate by making multiple copies of themselves through self-assembly. However, viruses do not metabolize and they require a host cell to make new products. Virus self-assembly within host cells has implications for the study of the origin of life, as it may support the hypothesis that life could have started as self-assembling organic molecules.[54][55][56]

Biophysics

Main article: Biophysics

To reflect the minimum phenomena required, other biological definitions of life have been proposed,[57] with many of these being based upon chemical systems. Biophysicists have commented that living things function on negative entropy.[58][59] In other words, living processes can be viewed as a delay of the spontaneous diffusion or dispersion of the internal energy of biological molecules towards more potential microstates.[17] In more detail, according to physicists such as John Bernal, Erwin Schrödinger, Eugene Wigner, and John Avery, life is a member of the class of phenomena that are open or continuous systems able to decrease their internal entropy at the expense of substances or free energy taken in from the environment and subsequently rejected in a degraded form.[60][61] The emergence and increasing popularity of biomimetics or biomimicry (the design and production of materials, structures, and systems that are modeled on biological entities and processes) will likely redefine the boundary between natural and artificial life.[62]

Living systems theories

Living systems are open self-organizing living things that interact with their environment. These systems are maintained by flows of information, energy, and matter.

Definition of cellular life according to Budisa, Kubyshkin and Schmidt.

Budisa, Kubyshkin and Schmidt defined cellular life as an organizational unit resting on four pillars/cornerstones: (i) energy, (ii) metabolism, (iii) information and (iv) form. This system is able to regulate and control metabolism and energy supply and contains at least one subsystem that functions as an information carrier (genetic information). Cells as self-sustaining units are parts of different populations that are involved in the unidirectional and irreversible open-ended process known as evolution.[63]

Some scientists have proposed in the last few decades that a general living systems theory is required to explain the nature of life.[64] Such a general theory would arise out of the ecological and biological sciences and attempt to map general principles for how all living systems work. Instead of examining phenomena by attempting to break things down into components, a general living systems theory explores phenomena in terms of dynamic patterns of the relationships of organisms with their environment.[65]

Gaia hypothesis

Main article: Gaia hypothesis

The idea that Earth is alive is found in philosophy and religion, but the first scientific discussion of it was by the

Scottish scientist James Hutton. In 1785, he stated that Earth was a superorganism and that its proper study should be physiology. Hutton is considered the father of geology, but his idea of a living Earth was forgotten in the intense reductionism of the 19th century.[66]:10 The Gaia hypothesis, proposed in the 1960s by scientist James Lovelock,[67][68] suggests that life on Earth functions as a single organism that defines and maintains environmental conditions necessary for its survival.[66] This hypothesis served as one of the foundations of the modern Earth system science.

Nonfractionability

Robert Rosen devoted a large part of his career, from 1958[69] onwards, to developing a comprehensive theory of life as a self-organizing complex system, "closed to efficient causation"[70] He defined a system component as "a unit of organization; a part with a function, i.e., a definite relation between part and whole." He identified the "nonfractionability of components in an organism" as the fundamental difference between living systems and "biological machines." He summarized his views in his book Life Itself.[71] Similar ideas may be found in the book Living Systems[72] by James Grier Miller.

Life as a property of ecosystems

A systems view of life treats environmental fluxes and biological fluxes together as a "reciprocity of influence,"[73] and a reciprocal relation with environment is arguably as important for understanding life as it is for understanding ecosystems. As Harold J. Morowitz (1992) explains it, life is a property of an ecological system rather than a single organism or species.[74] He argues that an ecosystemic definition of life is preferable to a strictly biochemical or physical one. Robert Ulanowicz (2009) highlights mutualism as the key to understand the systemic, order-generating behavior of life and ecosystems.[75]

Complex systems biology

Main article: Complex systems biology

See also: Mathematical biology

Complex systems biology (CSB) is a field of science that studies the emergence of complexity in functional organisms from the viewpoint of dynamic systems theory.[76] The latter is also often called systems biology and aims to understand the most fundamental aspects of life. A closely related approach to CSB and systems biology called relational biology is concerned mainly with understanding life processes in terms of the most important relations, and categories of such relations among the essential functional components of organisms; for multicellular organisms, this has been defined as "categorical biology", or a model representation of organisms as a category theory of biological relations, as well as an algebraic topology of the functional organization of living organisms in terms of their dynamic, complex networks of metabolic, genetic, and epigenetic processes and signaling pathways.[77][78] Alternative but closely related approaches focus on the interdependence of constraints, where constraints can be either molecular, such as enzymes, or macroscopic, such as the geometry of a bone or of the vascular system.[79]

Darwinian dynamic

Main article: Evolutionary dynamics

It has also been argued that the evolution of order in living systems and certain physical systems obeys a common fundamental principle termed the Darwinian dynamic.[80][81] The Darwinian dynamic was formulated by first considering how macroscopic order is generated in a simple non-biological system far from thermodynamic equilibrium, and then extending consideration to short, replicating RNA molecules. The underlying order-generating process was concluded to be basically similar for both types of systems.[80]

Operator theory

Another systemic definition called the operator theory proposes that "life is a general term for the presence of the typical closures found in organisms; the typical closures are a membrane and an autocatalytic set in the cell"[82] and that an organism is any system with an organisation that complies with an operator type that is at least as complex as the cell.[83][84][85][86] Life can also be modeled as a network of inferior negative feedbacks of regulatory mechanisms subordinated to a superior positive feedback formed by the potential of expansion and reproduction.[87]

History of study

Materialism

Main article: Materialism

Plant growth in the Hoh Rainforest

Herds of zebra and impala gathering on the Maasai Mara plain

An aerial photo of microbial mats around the Grand Prismatic Spring of Yellowstone National Park

Some of the earliest theories of life were materialist, holding that all that exists is matter, and that life is merely a complex form or arrangement of matter. Empedocles (430 BC) argued that everything in the universe is made up of a combination of four eternal "elements" or "roots of all": earth, water, air, and fire. All change is explained by the arrangement and rearrangement of these four elements. The various forms of life are caused by an appropriate mixture of elements.[88]

Democritus (460 BC) thought that the essential characteristic of life is having a soul (psyche). Like other ancient writers, he was attempting to explain what makes something a living thing. His explanation was that fiery atoms make a soul in exactly the same way atoms and void account for any other thing. He elaborates on fire because of the apparent connection between life and heat, and because fire moves.[89]

Plato's world of eternal and unchanging Forms, imperfectly represented in matter by a divine Artisan, contrasts sharply with the various mechanistic Weltanschauungen, of which atomism was, by the fourth century at least, the most prominent ... This debate persisted throughout the ancient world. Atomistic mechanism got a shot in the arm from Epicurus ... while the Stoics adopted a divine teleology ... The choice seems simple: either show how a structured, regular world could arise out of undirected processes, or inject intelligence into the system.[90]

— R.J. Hankinson, Cause and Explanation in Ancient Greek Thought

The mechanistic materialism that originated in ancient Greece was revived and revised by the French philosopher René Descartes (1596–1650), who held that animals and humans were assemblages of parts that together functioned as a machine. This idea was developed further by Julien Offray de La Mettrie (1709–1750) in his book L'Homme Machine.[91]

In the 19th century, the advances in cell theory in biological science encouraged this view. The evolutionary theory of Charles Darwin (1859) is a mechanistic explanation for the origin of species by means of natural selection.[92]

At the beginning of the 20th century Stéphane Leduc (1853–1939) promoted the idea that biological processes could be understood in terms of physics and chemistry, and that their growth resembled that of inorganic crystals immersed in solutions of sodium silicate. His ideas, set out in his book La biologie synthétique[93] was widely dismissed during his lifetime, but has incurred a resurgence of interest in the work of Russell, Barge and colleagues.[94]

Hylomorphism

Main article: Hylomorphism

The structure of the souls of plants, animals, and humans, according to Aristotle

Hylomorphism is a theory first expressed by the Greek philosopher Aristotle (322 BC). The application of hylomorphism to biology was important to Aristotle, and biology is extensively covered in his extant writings. In this view, everything in the material universe has both matter and form, and the form of a living thing is its soul (Greek psyche, Latin anima). There are three kinds of souls: the vegetative soul of plants, which causes them to grow and decay and nourish themselves, but does not cause motion and sensation; the animal soul, which causes animals to move and feel; and the rational soul, which is the source of consciousness and reasoning, which (Aristotle believed) is found only in man.[95] Each higher soul has all of the attributes of the lower ones. Aristotle believed that while matter can exist without form, form cannot exist without matter, and that therefore the soul cannot exist without the body.[96]

This account is consistent with teleological explanations of life, which account for phenomena in terms of purpose or goal-directedness. Thus, the whiteness of the polar bear's coat is explained by its purpose of camouflage. The direction of causality (from the future to the past) is in contradiction with the scientific evidence for natural selection, which explains the consequence in terms of a prior cause. Biological features are explained not by looking at future optimal results, but by looking at the past evolutionary history of a species, which led to the natural selection of the features in question.[97]

Spontaneous generation

Main article: Spontaneous generation

Spontaneous generation was the belief that living organisms can form without descent from similar organisms. Typically, the idea was that certain forms such as fleas could arise from inanimate matter such as dust or the supposed seasonal generation of mice and insects from mud or garbage.[98]

The theory of spontaneous generation was proposed by Aristotle,[99] who compiled and expanded the work of prior natural philosophers and the various ancient explanations of the appearance of organisms; it was considered the best explanation for two millennia. It was decisively dispelled by the experiments of Louis Pasteur in 1859, who expanded upon the investigations of predecessors such as Francesco Redi.[100][101] Disproof of the traditional ideas of spontaneous generation is no longer controversial among biologists.[102][103][104]

Vitalism

Main article: Vitalism

Vitalism is the belief that the life-principle is non-material. This originated with Georg Ernst Stahl (17th century), and remained popular until the middle of the 19th century. It appealed to philosophers such as Henri Bergson, Friedrich Nietzsche, and Wilhelm Dilthey,[105] anatomists like Xavier Bichat, and chemists like Justus von Liebig.[106] Vitalism included the idea that there was a fundamental difference between organic and inorganic material, and the belief that organic material can only be derived from living things. This was disproved in 1828, when Friedrich Wöhler prepared urea from inorganic materials.[107] This Wöhler synthesis is considered the starting point of modern organic chemistry. It is of historical significance because for the first time an organic compound was produced in inorganic reactions.[106]

During the 1850s, Hermann von Helmholtz, anticipated by Julius Robert von Mayer, demonstrated that no energy is lost in muscle movement, suggesting that there were no "vital forces" necessary to move a muscle.[108] These results led to the abandonment of scientific interest in vitalistic theories, especially after Buchner's demonstration that alcoholic fermentation could occur in cell-free extracts of yeast.[109] Nonetheless, the belief still exists in pseudoscientific theories such as homeopathy, which interprets diseases and sickness as caused by disturbances in a hypothetical vital force or life force.[110]

Origin

CHAPTER TWO

"PRC" redirect

"PRC" redirects here. For other uses, see PRC (disambiguation) and China (disambiguation).

China (Chinese: 中国; pinyin: Zhōngguó), officially the People's Republic of China (PRC; Chinese: 中华人民共和国; pinyin: Zhōnghuá Rénmín Gònghéguó), is a country in East Asia. It is the world's most populous country, with a population of more than 1.4 billion. China spans five geographical time zones and borders 14 different countries, the second most of any country in the world after Russia. Covering an area of approximately 9.6 million square kilometers (3,700,000 sq mi), it is the world's third or fourth largest country.[i] The country consists of 23 provinces,[j] five autonomous regions, four municipalities, and two Special Administrative Regions (Hong Kong and Macau). The national capital is Beijing.

China emerged as one of the world's first civilizations in the fertile basin of the Yellow River in the North China Plain. China was one of the world's foremost economic powers for most of the two millennia from the 1st until the 19th century. For millennia, China's political system was based on absolute hereditary monarchies, or dynasties, beginning with the semi-legendary Xia dynasty in the 21st century BCE. Since then, China has expanded, fractured, and re-unified numerous times. In the 3rd century BCE, the Qin reunited core China and established the first Chinese empire. The succeeding Han dynasty (206 BCE – 220 CE) saw some of the most advanced technology at that time, including papermaking and the compass, along with agricultural and medical improvements. The invention of gunpowder and movable type in the Tang dynasty (618–907) and Northern Song dynasty (960–1127) completed the Four Great Inventions. Tang culture spread widely in Asia, as the new Silk Road brought traders to as far as Mesopotamia and the Horn of Africa. The Qing dynasty, China's last dynasty, which formed the territorial basis for modern China, suffered heavy losses to foreign imperialism in the 19th century.

The Chinese monarchy collapsed in 1912 with the Xinhai Revolution, when the Republic of China (ROC) replaced the Qing dynasty. China was invaded by the Empire of Japan during World War II. The Civil War resulted in a division of territory in 1949 when the Chinese Communist Party (CCP) established the People's Republic of China on the mainland while the Kuomintang-led ROC government retreated to the island of Taiwan.[k] Both claim to be the sole legitimate government of China, although the United Nations has recognized the PRC as the sole representation since 1971. China conducted a series of economic reforms since 1978, and entered into the World Trade Organization in 2001.

China is currently governed as a unitary one-party socialist republic by the CCP. China is a permanent member of the United Nations Security Council and a founding member of several multilateral and regional cooperation organizations such as the Asian Infrastructure

Investment Bank, the Silk Road Fund, the New Development Bank, the Shanghai Cooperation Organization, and the RCEP, and is a member of the BRICS, the G8+5, the G20, the APEC, and the East Asia Summit. It ranks among the lowest in international measurements of civil liberties, government transparency, freedom of the press, freedom of religion and ethnic minorities. Chinese authorities have been criticized by political dissidents and human rights activists for widespread human rights abuses, including political repression, mass censorship, mass surveillance of their citizens and violent suppression of protests.

China is the world's largest economy by GDP at purchasing power parity, second-largest economy by nominal GDP, and the world's second wealthiest country by total wealth. The country has a fast growing major economy and is the world's largest manufacturer and exporter. China is a recognized nuclear-weapon state with the world's largest standing army by military personnel and second-largest defense budget.

ps

The word "China" has been used in English since the 16th century; however, it was not a word used by the Chinese themselves during this period. Its origin has been traced through Portuguese, Malay, and Persian back to the Sanskrit word Chīna, used in ancient India.[19] "China" appears in Richard Eden's 1555 translation[l] of the 1516 journal of the Portuguese explorer Duarte Barbosa.[m][19] Barbosa's usage was derived from Persian Chīn (چین), which was in turn derived from Sanskrit Cīna (चीन).[24] Cīna was first used in early Hindu scripture, including the Mahābhārata (5th century BCE) and the Laws of Manu (2nd century BCE).[25] In 1655, Martino Martini suggested that the word China is derived ultimately from the name of the Qin dynasty (221–206 BCE).[26][25] Although usage in Indian sources precedes this dynasty, this derivation is still given in various sources.[27] The origin of the Sanskrit word is a matter of debate, according to the Oxford English Dictionary.[19] Alternative suggestions include the names for Yelang and the Jing or Chu state.[25][28] The official name of the modern state is the "People's Republic of China" (simplified Chinese: 中华人民共和国; traditional Chinese: 中華人民共和國; pinyin: Zhōnghuá Rénmín Gònghéguó). The shorter form is "China" Zhōngguó (中国; 中國) from zhōng ("central") and guó ("state"),[n] a term which developed under the Western Zhou dynasty in reference to its royal demesne.[o] It was then applied to the area around Luoyi (present-day Luoyang) during the Eastern Zhou and then to China's Central Plain before being used as an occasional synonym for the state under the Qing.[30] It was often used as a cultural concept to distinguish the Huaxia people from perceived "barbarians".[30] The name Zhongguo is also translated as "Middle Kingdom" in English.[32] China (PRC) is sometimes referred to as the Mainland when distinguishing the ROC from the PRC.[33][34][35][36]

History

Main articles: History of China and Timeline of Chinese history

Prehistory

10,000 years old pottery, Xianren Cave culture (18000–7000 BCE)

Archaeological evidence suggests that early hominids inhabited China 2.25 million years ago.[37] The hominid fossils of Peking Man, a Homo erectus who used fire,[38] were discovered in a cave at Zhoukoudian near Beijing; they have been dated to between 680,000 and 780,000 years ago.[39] The fossilized teeth of Homo sapiens (dated to 125,000–80,000 years ago) have been discovered in Fuyan Cave in Dao County, Hunan.[40] Chinese proto-writing existed in Jiahu around 7000 BCE,[41] at Damaidi around 6000 BCE,[42] Dadiwan from 5800 to 5400 BCE, and Banpo dating from the 5th millennium BCE. Some scholars have suggested that the Jiahu symbols (7th millennium BCE) constituted the earliest Chinese writing system.[41]

Early dynastic rule

Further information: Three Sovereigns and Five Emperors, Xia dynasty, Shang dynasty, Zhou dynasty, Spring and Autumn period, and Warring States period

Yinxu, the ruins of the capital of the late Shang dynasty (14th century BCE)

According to Chinese tradition, the first dynasty was the Xia, which emerged around 2100 BCE.[43] The Xia dynasty marked the beginning of China's political system based on hereditary monarchies, or dynasties, which lasted for a millennium.[44] The dynasty was considered mythical by historians until scientific excavations found early Bronze Age sites at Erlitou, Henan in 1959.[45] It remains unclear whether these sites are the remains of the Xia dynasty or of another culture from the same period.[46] The succeeding Shang dynasty is the earliest to be confirmed by contemporary records.[47] The Shang ruled the plain of the Yellow River in eastern China from the 17th to the 11th century BCE.[48] Their oracle bone script (from c. 1500 BCE)[49][50] represents the oldest form of Chinese writing yet found[51] and is a direct ancestor of modern Chinese characters.[52]

The Shang was conquered by the Zhou, who ruled between the 11th and 5th centuries BCE, though centralized authority was slowly eroded by feudal warlords. Some principalities eventually emerged from the weakened Zhou, no longer fully obeyed the Zhou king, and continually waged war with each other in the 300-year Spring and Autumn period. By the time of the Warring States period of the 5th–3rd centuries BCE, there were only seven powerful states left.[53]

Imperial China

China's first emperor, Qin Shi Huang, is famed for having united the Warring States' walls to form the Great Wall of China. Most of the present structure, however, dates to the Ming dynasty.

The Warring States period ended in 221 BCE after the state of Qin conquered the other six kingdoms, reunited China and established the dominant order of autocracy. King Zheng of Qin proclaimed himself the First Emperor of the Qin dynasty. He enacted Qin's legalist reforms throughout China, notably the forced standardization of Chinese characters, measurements, road widths (i.e., cart axles' length), and currency. His dynasty also conquered the Yue tribes in Guangxi, Guangdong, and Vietnam.[54] The Qin dynasty lasted only fifteen years, falling soon after the First Emperor's death, as his harsh authoritarian policies led to widespread rebellion.[55][56]

Following a widespread civil war during which the imperial library at Xianyang was burned,[p] the Han dynasty emerged to rule China between 206 BCE and CE 220, creating a cultural identity among its populace still remembered in the ethnonym of the Han Chinese.[55][56] The Han expanded the empire's territory considerably, with military campaigns reaching Central Asia, Mongolia,

South Korea, and Yunnan, and the recovery of Guangdong and northern Vietnam from Nanyue. Han involvement in Central Asia and Sogdia helped establish the land route of the Silk Road, replacing the earlier path over the Himalayas to India. Han China gradually became the largest economy of the ancient world.[58] Despite the Han's initial decentralization and the official abandonment of the Qin philosophy of Legalism in favor of Confucianism, Qin's legalist institutions and policies continued to be employed by the Han government and its successors.[59]

Map showing the expansion of Han dynasty in the 2nd century BC

After the end of the Han dynasty, a period of strife known as Three Kingdoms followed,[60] whose central figures were later immortalized in one of the Four Classics of Chinese literature. At its end, Wei was swiftly overthrown by the Jin dynasty. The Jin fell to civil war upon the ascension of a developmentally disabled emperor; the Five Barbarians then invaded and ruled northern China as the Sixteen States. The Xianbei unified them as the Northern Wei, whose Emperor Xiaowen reversed his predecessors‘ apartheid policies and enforced a drastic sinification on his subjects, largely integrating them into Chinese culture. In the south, the general Liu Yu secured the abdication of the Jin in favor of the Liu Song. The various successors of these states became known as the Northern and Southern dynasties, with the two areas finally reunited by the Sui in 581. The Sui restored the Han to power through China, reformed its agriculture, economy and imperial examination system, constructed the Grand Canal, and patronized Buddhism. However, they fell quickly when their conscription for public works and a failed war in northern Korea provoked widespread unrest.[61][62]

Under the succeeding Tang and Song dynasties, Chinese economy, technology, and culture entered a golden age.[63] The Tang Empire retained control of the Western Regions and the Silk Road,[64] which brought traders to as far as Mesopotamia and the Horn of Africa,[65] and made the capital Chang'an a cosmopolitan urban center. However, it was devastated and weakened by the An Lushan Rebellion in the 8th century.[66] In 907, the Tang disintegrated completely when the local military governors became ungovernable. The Song dynasty ended the separatist situation in 960, leading to a balance of power between the Song and Khitan Liao. The Song was the first government in world history to issue paper money and the first Chinese polity to establish a permanent standing navy which was supported by the developed shipbuilding industry along with the sea trade.[67]

The Tang dynasty at its greatest extent

A detail from Along the River During the Qingming Festival, a 12th-century painting showing everyday life in the Song dynasty's capital, Bianjing (present-day Kaifeng)

Between the 10th and 11th centuries, the population of China doubled in size to around 100 million people, mostly because of the expansion of rice cultivation in central and southern China, and the production of abundant food surpluses. The Song dynasty also saw a revival of Confucianism, in response to the growth of Buddhism during the Tang,[68] and a flourishing of philosophy and the arts, as landscape art and porcelain were brought to new levels of maturity and complexity.[69][70] However, the military weakness of the Song army was observed by the Jurchen Jin dynasty. In 1127, Emperor Huizong of Song and the capital Bianjing were captured during the Jin–Song

Wars. The remnants of the Song retreated to southern China.[71]

The Mongol conquest of China began in 1205 with the gradual conquest of Western Xia by Genghis Khan,[72] who also invaded Jin territories.[73] In 1271, the Mongol leader Kublai Khan established the Yuan dynasty, which conquered the last remnant of the Song dynasty in 1279. Before the Mongol invasion, the population of Song China was 120 million citizens; this was reduced to 60 million by the time of the census in 1300.[74] A peasant named Zhu Yuanzhang led a rebellion that overthrew the Yuan in 1368 and founded the Ming dynasty as the Hongwu Emperor. Under the Ming dynasty, China enjoyed another golden age, developing one of the strongest navies in the world and a rich and prosperous economy amid a flourishing of art and culture. It was during this period that admiral Zheng He led the Ming treasure voyages throughout the Indian Ocean, reaching as far as East Africa.[75]

The Qing conquest of the Ming and expansion of the empire

In the early years of the Ming dynasty, China's capital was moved from Nanjing to Beijing. With the budding of capitalism, philosophers such as Wang Yangming further critiqued and expanded Neo-Confucianism with concepts of individualism and equality of four occupations.[76] The scholar-official stratum became a supporting force of industry and commerce in the tax boycott movements, which, together with the famines and defense against Japanese invasions of Korea (1592–1598) and Manchu invasions led to an exhausted treasury.[77] In 1644, Beijing was captured by a coalition of peasant rebel forces led by Li Zicheng. The Chongzhen Emperor committed suicide when the city fell. The Manchu Qing dynasty, then allied with Ming dynasty general Wu Sangui, overthrew Li's short-lived Shun dynasty and subsequently seized control of Beijing, which became the new capital of the Qing dynasty.[citation needed]

The Qing dynasty, which lasted from 1644 until 1912, was the last imperial dynasty of China. Its conquest of the Ming (1618–1683) cost 25 million lives and the economy of China shrank drastically.[78] After the Southern Ming ended, the further conquest of the Dzungar Khanate added Mongolia, Tibet and Xinjiang to the empire.[79] The centralized autocracy was strengthened to suppress anti-Qing sentiment with the policy of valuing agriculture and restraining commerce, the Haijin ("sea ban"), and ideological control as represented by the literary inquisition, causing social and technological stagnation.[80][81]

Fall of the Qing dynasty

Further information: Century of humiliation, Opium Wars, First Sino-Japanese War, and Boxer Rebellion

The Eight-Nation Alliance invaded China to defeat the anti-foreign Boxers and their Qing backers. The image shows a celebration ceremony inside the Chinese imperial palace, the Forbidden City after the signing of the Boxer Protocol in 1901.

In the mid-19th century, the Qing dynasty experienced Western imperialism in the Opium Wars with Britain and France. China was forced to pay compensation, open treaty ports, allow extraterritoriality for foreign nationals, and cede Hong Kong to the British[82] under the 1842 Treaty of Nanking, the first of the Unequal Treaties. The First Sino-Japanese War (1894–1895) resulted in Qing China's loss of influence in the Korean Peninsula, as well as the cession of Taiwan to Japan.[83] The Qing dynasty also began experiencing internal unrest in which tens of millions of people died, especially in the White Lotus Rebellion, the failed Taiping Rebellion that ravaged southern China in the 1850s and 1860s and the Dungan Revolt (1862–1877) in the northwest. The initial success of the Self-Strengthening Movement of the 1860s was frustrated by a series of military defeats in the 1880s and 1890s.[citation needed]

In the 19th century, the great Chinese diaspora began. Losses due to emigration were added to by conflicts and catastrophes such as the Northern Chinese Famine of 1876–1879, in which between 9 and 13 million people died.[84] The Guangxu Emperor drafted a reform plan in 1898 to establish a modern constitutional monarchy, but these plans were thwarted by the Empress Dowager Cixi. The ill-fated anti-foreign Boxer Rebellion of 1899–1901 further weakened the dynasty. Although Cixi sponsored a program of reforms, the Xinhai Revolution of 1911–1912 brought an end to the Qing dynasty and established the Republic of China.[85] Puyi, the last Emperor of China, abdicated in 1912.[86]

Establishment of the Republic and World War II

Main article: Republic of China (1912–1949)

Further information: 1911 Revolution, Second Sino-Japanese War, Chinese Civil War, and Chinese Communist Revolution

Sun Yat-sen, the founding father of Republic of China, the first republic in Asia.

On 1 January 1912, the Republic of China was established, and Sun Yat-sen of the Kuomintang (the KMT or Nationalist Party) was proclaimed provisional president.[87] On 12 February 1912, regent Empress Dowager Longyu sealed the imperial abdication decree on behalf of 4 year old Puyi, the last emperor of China, ending 5,000 years of monarchy in China.[88] In March 1912, the presidency was given to Yuan Shikai, a former Qing general who in 1915 proclaimed himself Emperor of China. In the face of popular condemnation and opposition from his own Beiyang Army, he was forced to abdicate and re-establish the republic in 1916.[89]

After Yuan Shikai's death in 1916, China was politically fragmented. Its Beijing-based government was internationally recognized but virtually powerless; regional warlords controlled most of its territory.[90][91] In the late 1920s, the Kuomintang under Chiang Kai-shek, the then Principal of the Republic of China Military Academy, was able to reunify the country under its own control with a series of deft military and political maneuverings, known collectively as the Northern Expedition.[92][93] The Kuomintang moved the nation's capital to Nanjing and implemented "political tutelage", an intermediate stage of political development outlined in Sun Yat-sen's San-min program for transforming China into a modern democratic state.[94][95] The political division in China made it difficult for Chiang to battle the communist-led People's Liberation Army (PLA), against whom the Kuomintang had been warring since 1927 in the Chinese Civil War. This war continued successfully for the Kuomintang, especially after the PLA retreated in the Long March, until Japanese aggression and the 1936 Xi'an Incident forced Chiang to confront Imperial Japan.[96]

Chiang Kai-shek and Mao Zedong toasting together in 1945 following the end of World War II

The Second Sino-Japanese War (1937–1945), a theater of World War II, forced an uneasy alliance between the Kuomintang and the Communists. Japanese forces committed numerous war atrocities against the civilian population; in all, as many as 20 million Chinese civilians died.[97] An estimated 40,000 to 300,000 Chinese were massacred in the city of Nanjing alone during the Japanese occupation.[98] During the war, China, along with the UK, the United States, and the Soviet Union, were referred to as "trusteeship of the powerful"[99] and were recognized as the Allied "Big Four" in the Declaration by United Nations.[100][101] Along with the other three great powers, China was one of the four major Allies of World War II, and was later considered one of the primary victors in the war.[102][103] After the surrender of Japan in 1945, Taiwan, including the Pescadores, was returned to Chinese control. China emerged victorious but war-ravaged and financially drained. The continued distrust between the Kuomintang and the Communists led to the resumption of civil war. Constitutional rule was established in 1947, but because of the ongoing unrest, many provisions of the ROC constitution were never implemented in mainland China.[104]

Civil War and the People's Republic

Main article: History of the People's Republic of China

Further information: Proclamation of the People's Republic of China, Retreat of the government of the Republic of China to Taiwan, and Cultural Revolution

Mao Zedong proclaiming the establishment of the PRC in 1949.

CHAPTER THREE

Major com

Major combat in the Chinese Civil War ended in 1949 with the CCP gain control of most of mainland China, and the Kuomintang retreating offshore to Taiwan, reducing its territory to only Taiwan, Hainan, and their surrounding islands. On 1 October 1949, CCP Chairman Mao Zedong formally proclaimed the establishment of the People's Republic of China at the new nation's founding ceremony and inaugural military parade in Tiananmen Square, Beijing.[105][106] In 1950, the People's Liberation Army captured Hainan from the ROC[107] and incorporated Tibet.[108] However, remaining Kuomintang forces continued to wage an insurgency in western China throughout the 1950s.[109]

The government consolidated its popularity among the peasants through land reform, which included the execution of between 1 and 2 million landlords.[110] China developed an independent industrial system and its own nuclear weapons.[111] The Chinese population increased from 550 million in 1950 to 900 million in 1974.[112] However, the Great Leap Forward, an idealistic massive reform project, resulted in an estimated 15 to 35 million deaths between 1958 and 1961, mostly from starvation.[113][114] In 1966, Mao and his allies launched the Cultural Revolution, sparking a decade of political recrimination and social upheaval that lasted until Mao's death in 1976. In October 1971, the PRC replaced the Republic of China in the United Nations, and took its seat as a permanent member of the Security Council.[115]

Reforms and contemporary history

Further information: Chinese economic reform

After Mao's death, the Gang of Four was quickly arrested by Hua Guofeng and held responsible for the excesses of the Cultural Revolution. Elder Deng Xiaoping took power in 1978, and instituted significant economic reforms. The CCP loosened governmental control over citizens' personal lives, and the communes were gradually disbanded in favor of working contracted to households. This marked China's transition from a planned economy to a mixed economy with an increasingly open-market environment.[116] China adopted its current constitution on 4 December 1982. In 1989, the suppression of student protests in Tiananmen Square brought condemnations and sanctions against the Chinese government from various foreign countries.[117]

Jiang Zemin, Li Peng and Zhu Rongji led the nation in the 1990s. Under their administration, China's economic performance pulled an estimated[by whom?] 150 million peasants out of poverty and sustained an average annual gross domestic product growth rate of 11.2%.[118][better source needed] British Hong Kong and Portuguese Macau returned to China in 1997 and 1999, respectively, as the Hong Kong and Macau special administrative regions under the principle of One Country, Two Systems. The country joined the World Trade Organization in 2001, and maintained its high rate of economic growth under Hu Jintao and Wen Jiabao's leadership in the 2000s. However, the growth also severely impacted the country's resources and environment,[119][120] and caused major social displacement.[121][122]

Chinese Communist Party general secretary Xi Jinping has ruled since 2012 and has pursued large-scale efforts to reform China's economy [123][124] (which has suffered from structural instabilities and slowing growth),[125][126][127] and has also reformed the one-child policy and penal system,[128] as well as instituting a vast anti corruption crackdown.[129] In 2013, China initiated the Belt and Road Initiative, a global infrastructure investment project.[130]

On 1 July 2021, the People's Republic of China celebrated the 100th anniversary of the establishment of the CCP (first of the Two Centenaries) with a huge gathering in Tiananmen Square and cultural artistic performance in Beijing National Stadium in Beijing.[131]

Geography

Main article: Geography of China

Satellite image of China from NASA WorldWind

China's landscape is vast and diverse, ranging from the Gobi and Taklamakan Deserts in the arid north to the subtropical forests in the wetter south. The Himalaya, Karakoram, Pamir and Tian Shan mountain ranges separate China from much of South and Central Asia. The Yangtze and Yellow Rivers, the third- and sixth-longest in the world, respectively, run from the Tibetan Plateau to the densely populated eastern seaboard. China's coastline along the Pacific Ocean is 14,500 km (9,000 mi) long and is bounded by the Bohai, Yellow, East China and South China seas. China connects through the Kazakh border to the Eurasian Steppe which has been an artery of communication between East and West since the Neolithic through the

Steppe route – the ancestor of the terrestrial Silk Road(s).[citation needed]

The territory of China lies between latitudes 18° and 54° N, and longitudes 73° and 135° E. The geographical center of China is marked by the Center of the Country Monument at 35°50′40.9″N 103°27′7.5″E. China's landscapes vary significantly across its vast territory. In the east, along the shores of the Yellow Sea and the East China Sea, there are extensive and densely populated alluvial plains, while on the edges of the Inner Mongolian plateau in the north, broad grasslands predominate. Southern China is dominated by hills and low mountain ranges, while the central-east hosts the deltas of China's two major rivers, the Yellow River and the Yangtze River. Other major rivers include the Xi, Mekong, Brahmaputra and Amur. To the west sit major mountain ranges, most notably the Himalayas. High plateaus feature among the more arid landscapes of the north, such as the Taklamakan and the Gobi Desert. The world's highest point, Mount Everest (8,848 m), lies on the Sino-Nepalese border.[132] The country's lowest point, and the world's third-lowest, is the dried lake bed of Ayding Lake (−154 m) in the Turpan Depression.[133]

Climate

Further information: Great Green Wall (China)

Köppen-Geiger climate classification map for mainland China.[134]

China's climate is mainly dominated by dry seasons and wet monsoons, which lead to pronounced temperature differences between winter and summer. In the winter, northern winds coming from high-latitude areas are cold and dry; in summer, southern winds from coastal areas at lower latitudes are warm and moist.[135]

A major environmental issue in China is the continued expansion of its deserts, particularly the Gobi Desert.[136][137] Although barrier tree lines planted since the 1970s have reduced the frequency of sandstorms, prolonged drought and poor agricultural practices have resulted in dust storms plaguing northern China each spring, which then spread to other parts of East Asia, including Japan and Korea. China's environmental watchdog, SEPA, stated in 2007 that China is losing 4,000 km2 (1,500 sq mi) per year to desertification.[138] Water quality, erosion, and pollution control have become important issues in China's relations with other countries. Melting glaciers in the Himalayas could potentially lead to water shortages for hundreds of millions of people.[139] According to academics, in order to limit climate change in China to 1.5 °C (2.7 °F) electricity generation from coal in China without carbon capture must be phased out by 2045.[140] Official government statistics about Chinese agricultural productivity are considered unreliable, due to exaggeration of production at subsidiary government levels.[141][142] Much of China has a climate very suitable for agriculture and the country has been the world's largest producer of rice, wheat, tomatoes, eggplant, grapes, watermelon, spinach, and many other crops.[143]

Biodiversity

Main article: Wildlife of China

A giant panda, China's most famous endangered and endemic species, at the Chengdu Research Base of Giant Panda Breeding in Sichuan

China is one of 17 megadiverse countries,[144] lying in two of the world's major biogeographic realms: the Palearctic and the Indomalayan. By one measure, China has over 34,687 species of animals and vascular plants, making it the third-most biodiverse country in the world, after Brazil and Colombia.[145] The country signed the Rio de Janeiro Convention on Biological Diversity on 11 June 1992, and became a party to the convention on 5 January 1993.[146] It later produced a National Biodiversity Strategy and Action Plan, with one revision that was received by the convention on 21 September 2010.[147]

China is home to at least 551 species of mammals (the third-highest such number in the world),[148] 1,221 species of birds (eighth),[149] 424 species of reptiles (seventh)[150] and 333 species of amphibians (seventh).[151] Wildlife in China shares habitat with, and bears acute pressure from, the world's largest population of humans. At least 840 animal species are threatened, vulnerable or in danger of local extinction in China, due mainly to human activity such as habitat destruction, pollution and poaching for food, fur and ingredients for traditional Chinese medicine.[152] Endangered wildlife is protected by law, and as of 2005, the country has over 2,349 nature reserves, covering a total area of 149.95 million hectares, 15 percent of China's total land area.[153][better source needed] Most wild animals have been eliminated from the core agricultural regions of east and central China, but they have fared better in the mountainous south and west.[154][155] The Baiji was confirmed extinct on 12 December 2006.[156]

China has over 32,000 species of vascular plants,[157] and is home to a variety of forest types. Cold coniferous forests predominate in the north of the country, supporting animal species such as moose and Asian black bear, along with over 120 bird species.[158] The understory of moist conifer forests may contain thickets of bamboo. In higher montane stands of juniper and yew, the bamboo is replaced by rhododendrons. Subtropical forests, which are predominate in central and southern China, support a high density of plant species including numerous rare endemics. Tropical and seasonal rainforests, though confined to Yunnan and Hainan Island, contain a quarter of all the animal and plant species found in China.[158] China has over 10,000 recorded species of fungi,[159] and of them, nearly 6,000 are higher fungi.[160]

Environment

Main articles: Environment of China and Environmental issues in China

See also: Renewable energy in China, Water resources of China, Energy policy of China, and Climate change in China

The Three Gorges Dam is the largest hydroelectric dam in the world.

In the early 2000s, China has suffered from environmental deterioration and pollution due to its rapid pace of industrialization.[161][162] While regulations such as the 1979 Environmental Protection Law are fairly stringent, they are poorly enforced, as they are frequently disregarded by local communities and government officials in favor of rapid economic development.[163] China is the country with the second highest death toll because of air pollution, after India. There are approximately 1 million deaths caused by exposure to ambient air pollution.[164][165] Although China ranks as the highest CO2 emitting country in the world,[166] it only emits 8 tons of CO2 per capita, significantly lower than developed countries such as the United States (16.1), Australia (16.8) and South Korea (13.6).[167]

In recent years, China has clamped down on pollution. In March 2014, CCP General Secretary Xi Jinping "declared war" on pollution during the opening of the National People's Congress.[168] After extensive debate lasting nearly two years, the parliament approved a new environmental law in April. The new law empowers environmental enforcement agencies with great punitive power and large fines for offenders, defines areas which require extra protection, and gives independent environmental groups more ability to operate in the country.[citation needed] In 2020, Chinese Communist Party general secretary Xi Jinping announced that China aims to peak emissions before 2030 and go carbon-neutral by 2060 in accordance with the Paris climate accord.[169] According to Climate Action Tracker, if accomplished it would lower the expected rise in global temperature by 0.2 - 0.3 degrees - "the biggest single reduction ever estimated by the Climate Action Tracker".[170] In September 2021 Xi Jinping announced that China will not build "coal-fired power projects abroad". The decision can be "pivotal" in reducing emissions. The Belt and Road Initiative did not include financing such projects already in the first half of 2021.[171]

The country also had significant water pollution problems: 8.2% of China's rivers had been polluted by industrial and agricultural waste in 2019.[172][173] China had a 2018 Forest Landscape Integrity Index mean score of 7.14/10, ranking it 53rd globally out of 172 countries.[174] In 2020, a sweeping law was passed by the Chinese government to protect the ecology of the Yangtze River. The new laws include strengthening ecological protection rules for hydropower projects along the river, banning chemical plants within 1 kilometer of the river, relocating polluting industries, severely restricting sand mining as well as a complete fishing ban on all the natural waterways of the river, including all its major tributaries and lakes.[175]

China is also the world's leading investor in renewable energy and its commercialization, with $52 billion invested in 2011 alone;[176][177][178] it is a major manufacturer of renewable energy technologies and invests heavily in local-scale renewable energy projects.[179][180][181] By 2015, over 24% of China's energy was derived from renewable sources, while most notably from hydroelectric power: a total installed capacity of 197 GW makes China the largest hydroelectric power producer in the world.[182][183] China also has the largest power capacity of installed solar photovoltaics system and wind power system in the world.[184][185] Greenhouse gas emissions by China are the world's largest,[167] as is renewable energy in China.[186]

Political geography

Main articles: Borders of China, Coastline of China, and Territorial changes of the People's Republic of China

Map showing the territorial claims of the PRC.

The People's Republic of China is the second-largest country in the world by land area after Russia.[q][r] China's total area is generally stated as being approximately 9,600,000 km2 (3,700,000 sq mi).[187][better source needed] Specific area figures range from 9,572,900 km2 (3,696,100 sq mi) according to the Encyclopædia Britannica,[188] to 9,596,961 km2 (3,705,407 sq mi) according to the UN Demographic Yearbook,[5] and the CIA World Factbook.[8]

China has the longest combined land border in the world, measuring 22,117 km (13,743 mi) and its coastline covers approximately 14,500 km (9,000 mi) from the mouth of the Yalu River (Amnok River) to the Gulf of Tonkin.[8] China borders 14 nations and extends across much of East Asia, bordering Vietnam, Laos, and Myanmar (Burma) in Southeast Asia; India, Bhutan, Nepal, Afghanistan, and Pakistan[s] in South Asia; Tajikistan, Kyrgyzstan and Kazakhstan in Central Asia; and Russia, Mongolia, and North Korea in Inner Asia and Northeast Asia. Additionally, China shares maritime boundaries with South Korea, Japan, Vietnam, and the Philippines.[citation needed]

Politics

Main article: Politics of China

See also: List of current Chinese provincial leaders

The Great Hall of the People
where the National People's Congress convenes

The Zhongnanhai, headquarters of the Chinese government and Chinese Communist Party.

The Chinese constitution states that The People's Republic of China "is a socialist state governed by a people's democratic dictatorship that is led by the working class and based on an alliance of workers and peasants," and that the state institutions "shall practice the principle of democratic centralism."[189] The PRC is one of the world's only socialist states governed by a communist party. The Chinese government has been variously described as communist and socialist, but also as authoritarian[190] and corporatist,[191] with heavy restrictions in many areas, most notably against free access to the Internet, freedom of the press, freedom of assembly, the right to have children, free formation of social organizations and freedom of religion.[192] Its current political, ideological and economic system has been termed by its leaders as a "consultative democracy" "people's democratic dictatorship", "socialism with Chinese characteristics" (which is Marxism adapted to Chinese circumstances) and the "socialist market economy" respectively.[193][194]

Communist Party

Main article: Chinese Communist Party

See also: United Front (China) and Generations of Chinese leadership

The Chinese Communist Party is the founding and ruling political party of China.

Since 2018, the main body of the Chinese constitution declares that "the defining feature of socialism with Chinese characteristics is the leadership of the Chinese Communist Party (CCP)."[195] The 2018 amendments constitutionalized the de facto one-party state status of China,[195] wherein the CCP General Secretary (party leader) holds ultimate power and authority over state and government and serves as the informal Paramount leader.[196] The current General Secretary is Xi Jinping, who took office on 15 November 2012, and was re-elected on 25 October 2017.[197] The electoral system is pyramidal. Local People's Congresses are directly elected, and higher levels of People's Congresses up to the National People's Congress (NPC) are indirectly elected by the People's Congress of the level immediately below.[189]

This section relies too much on references to primary sources. Please improve this section by adding secondary or tertiary sources. (November 2020) (Learn how and when to remove this template message)

Another eight political parties, have representatives in the NPC and the Chinese People's Political Consultative Conference (CPPCC).[198] China supports the Leninist principle of "democratic centralism",[189] but critics describe the elected National People's Congress as a "rubber stamp" body.[199]

Since both the CCP and the People's Liberation Army (PLA) promote according to seniority, it is possible to discern distinct generations of Chinese leadership.[200] In official discourse, each group of leadership is identified with a distinct extension of the ideology of the party. Historians have studied various periods in the development of the government of the People's Republic of China by reference to these "generations".

Further information: Generations of Chinese leadership

Generations of Chinese Leadership[200]

GenerationParamount leaderStartEndTheory

FirstMao Zedong19491976Mao Zedong Thought

Hua Guofeng19761978Two Whatevers

SecondDeng Xiaoping19781989Deng Xiaoping Theory

ThirdJiang Zemin19892002Three Represents

FourthHu Jintao20022012Scientific Outlook on Development

FifthXi Jinping2012Xi Jinping Thought

Government

Main article: Government of China

See also: List of national leaders of the People's Republic of China

Xi Jinping

CCP General Secretary and President

Li Keqiang

Premier

Li Zhanshu

Congress Chairman

China is a one-party state led by the Chinese Communist Party (CCP). The National People's Congress in 2018 altered the country's constitution to remove the two-term limit on holding the Presidency of China, permitting the current leader, Xi Jinping, to remain president of China (and General Secretary of the Chinese Communist Party) for an unlimited time, earning criticism for creating dictatorial governance.[201][202] The President is the titular head of state, elected by the National People's Congress. The Premier is the head of government, presiding over the State Council composed of four vice premiers and the heads of ministries and commissions. The incumbent president is Xi Jinping, who is also the General Secretary of the Chinese Communist Party and the Chairman of the Central Military Commission, making him China's paramount leader. The incumbent premier is Li Keqiang, who is also a senior member of the CCP Politburo Standing Committee, China's de facto top decision-making body.[203][204]

In 2017, Xi called on the communist party to further tighten its grip on the country, to uphold the unity of the party leadership, and achieve the "Chinese Dream of national rejuvenation".[193][205] Political concerns in China include the growing gap between rich and poor and government corruption.[206] Nonetheless, the level of public support for the government and its management of the nation is high, with 80–95% of Chinese citizens expressing satisfaction with the central government, according to a 2011 survey.[207] A 2020 survey from the Canadian Institutes of Health Research also found that 75% of Chinese were satisfied with the government on information dissemination amidst the COVID-19 pandemic, while 67% were satisfied with its delivery of daily necessities.[208][209]

Administrative divisions

Main articles: Administrative divisions of China, Districts of Hong Kong, and Municipalities and parishes of Macau

The People's Republic of China is officially divided into 23 provinces,[210] five autonomous regions (each with a designated minority group), and four municipalities—collectively referred to as "mainland China"—as well as the special administrative regions (SARs) of Hong Kong and Macau. Geographically, all 31 provincial divisions of mainland China can be grouped into six regions: North China, Northeast China, East China, South Central China, Southwest China, and Northwest China.[211]

China considers Taiwan to be its 23rd province,[210] although Taiwan is governed by the Republic of China (ROC), which rejects the PRC's claim. Conversely, the ROC constitution claims sovereignty over all divisions governed by the PRC.[212]

Printed by Libri Plureos GmbH in Hamburg, Germany

9 798886 410853